For Alison, with lots of Christmassy thanks – **M.S.**   For my mum – **S.C.**

BLOOMSBURY CHILDREN'S BOOKS
Bloomsbury Publishing Plc
50 Bedford Square, London, WC1B 3DP, UK
29 Earlsfort Terrace, Dublin 2, Ireland

BLOOMSBURY, BLOOMSBURY CHILDREN'S BOOKS and the Diana logo
are trademarks of Bloomsbury Publishing Plc

First published in Great Britain 2021 by Bloomsbury Publishing Plc

Text copyright © Mark Sperring 2021
Illustrations copyright © Sophie Corrigan 2021

Mark Sperring and Sophie Corrigan have asserted their rights under the Copyright,
Designs and Patents Act, 1988, to be identified as the Author and Illustrator of this work

A catalogue record for this book is available from the British Library

ISBN 978 1 5266 3680 5 (HB)
ISBN 978 1 5266 3681 2 (PB)
ISBN 978 1 5266 3679 9 (eBook)

1 3 5 7 9 10 8 6 4 2

Printed and bound in China by Leo Paper Products, Heshan, Guangdong

To find out more about our authors and books visit www.bloomsbury.com and sign up for our newsletters

JINGLE SMELLS

Mark SPERRING ❄ Sophie CORRIGAN

BLOOMSBURY
CHILDREN'S BOOKS
LONDON OXFORD NEW YORK NEW DELHI SYDNEY

Late one snowy Christmas Eve,
a skunk strolled into town
to see the bright and shiny lights
that twinkled all around.

But as he skipped
across the bridge,
a rather pungent smell

made a robin

FALL

DOWN

FLAT

and a snowman turn quite pale.

That little skunk named Jingle
gave a STINKY sigh.

"It's best," he said,
"to **hold
your nose**
whenever I pass by."

But just a few steps later,
a tree in the old town square
was overwhelmed by

Jingle smells

and

TEETERED

in the air.

The tree **fell** in the snow.

That little skunk named Jingle
looked at what he'd done . . .

"I think I've **ruined** Christmas,
for each and every one..."

And he might
have headed home

with a sad and sorry yelp...

if a reindeer on the rooftop
had not cried out for

HELP!

Springing

into action,

Jingle scaled

a towering wall,

climbing

EVER

higher

with no fear

that he

might fall.

But when he reached the rooftop
Jingle gasped in great dismay.
He saw . . .

Robbers!

Stolen presents!

Santa **tied up** in his sleigh!

"Quick!" called Santa desperately,
"Do something – do it fast!"

So Jingle gave
those villains an

EXTRA
STINKY
BLAST!

THUD and SPLAT!

They passed out in the snow!

That little skunk named Jingle looked at what he'd done . . .

"I think I've just **saved Christmas**,
for EACH and EVERY ONE!"

When the robbers had recovered,
they looked quite a shame-faced sight,
and they said, "We're **truly** sorry,
can we PLEASE help put things right?"

So they climbed down from the rooftop,
and did what they were told . . .

Who'd have thought
a STINKY night
would end such
a lovely way . . . .

And soon the
fallen Christmas tree
stood **SHIMMERING**
like gold!

"You're our
WHIFFY
Christmas hero!"
the reindeer cheered and roared.
While Jingle gave a smelly bow
and basked in sweet applause.

But, with presents to deliver, Santa said,
"It's time to fly!"

And then,
FOR **ONE NIGHT ONLY**...

A SKUNK TOOK TO THE SKY!

Jingle chuckled, "MERRY CHRISTMAS,"
to the twinkling town below
and called out, very wisely...

"Don't forget to hold your nose!"

CODE: STEM

ROBOTS

Real-world coding projects made fun

Max Wainewright

WAYLAND
www.waylandbooks.co.uk

First published in Great Britain in 2019
by Wayland

Text copyright © ICT Apps, 2019
Art and design copyright © Hodder and
Stoughton, 2019
All rights reserved

Credits:
Editor: Elise Short
Designer: Matt Lilly
Cover Design: Peter Scoulding
Illustrations: John Haslam

Every attempt has been made to clear copyright.
Should there be any inadvertent omission please
apply to the publisher for rectification.

HB ISBN: 978 1 5263 0835 1
PB ISBN: 978 1 5263 0836 8

Printed and bound in China

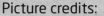

FSC
www.fsc.org
MIX
Paper from
responsible sources
FSC® C104740

Picture credits:
Shutterstock: NicoElNino 6, VCoscaron 12,
petrmalinak 14, Andrey_Popov 18, Sean Pavone 24,
Photographicss 28, Dreamstime: GarcÃa Juan 26.

Wayland
An imprint of
Hachette Children's Group
Part of Hodder and Stoughton
Carmelite House
50 Victoria Embankment
London EC4Y 0DZ

An Hachette UK Company
www.hachette.co.uk
www.hachettechildrens.co.uk

We recommend that children are supervised at all times when using the Internet.
Some of the projects in this series use a computer webcam or microphone. Please
make sure children are made aware that they should only allow a computer to access
the webcam or microphone on specific websites that a trusted adult has told them to
use. We do not recommend children use websites or microphones on any other
websites other than those mentioned in this book.

The website addresses (URLs) included in this book were valid at the time of going to press. However, it is possible that contents or
addresses may have changed since the publication of this book. No responsibility for any such changes can be accepted by either the author
or the Publisher.

Scratch is developed by the Lifelong Kindergarten Group at the MIT Media Lab. See http://scratch.mit.edu
Images and illustrations from Scratch included in this book have been developed by the Lifelong Kindergarten Group at the MIT Media Lab
(see http://scratch.mit.edu) and made available under the Creative Commons Attribution-ShareAlike 2.0 licence (https://creativecommons.org/
licenses/by-sa/2.0/deed.en). The third party trademarks used in this book are the property of their respective owners, including the Scratch
name and logo. The owners of these trademarks have not endorsed, authorised or sponsored this book.

Contents

Introduction

For thousands of years people have created machines that could carry out tasks to help us. In the 18th century inventors created 'automatons' – mechanical devices made to look like humans. These were able to carry out a series of movements or play a basic tune on an instrument. Relying on complex systems of gears and levers, these early robots were mainly used as a form of entertainment. It wasn't until the 1940s and 1950s that electronics was used to control and program robots. This led to the development of more and more sophisticated robots.

In this book we'll look at how the different systems within robots work, such as how they move around, sense where they are and interact with us. You'll use the algorithms and ideas that control real robots to create your own on-screen robots. These programs will help you understand how they work – and help you understand the world of robots.

There are lots of different ways to create code. We will be using a website called Scratch to do our coding.

Type **scratch.mit.edu** into your web browser, then click Create to start a new project.

Let's start by looking at the important parts of the screen in Scratch:

File Menu (for logged-in users)
If you want to you can create an account for free and save your work online. Check with a grown-up first. Alternatively you can use the Upload and Download options to save and open work on your computer.

Sound Library
Add sounds to your program from here.

New
Save Now
Save as a Copy
Go to My Stuff
Upload to your computer
Download to your computer
Record and Export Video
Revert

File Menu (for general users)
Choose upload and download to save and open work on your computer.

New
Upload from your computer
Download to your computer
Revert

All | Animals | Effects | Loops | Notes | Percussion

A Bass | A Elec Bass | A Elec Guitar | A Elec Piano
A Minor Uk... | A Piano | A Sax | A Trombone

File | Edit | Tutorials

Code | Costumes | Sounds

Block Categories
Choose commands from these categories, or just scroll through all.

Motion
Looks
Sound
Events
Control
Sensing
Operators
Variables
My Blocks

Motion
move 10 steps
turn 15 degrees
turn 15 degrees
go to random position
go to x: 0 y: 0
glide 1 secs to random position
glide 1 secs to x: 0 y: 0
point in direction 90
point towards mouse-pointer
change x by 10
set x to 0
change y by 10
set y to 0

Scripts Area
Add your commands or code here.

The Stage
Your program takes place here.

Sprites
Objects that move around in Scratch are called sprites.

Sprite1

Sprite1

Stage

Backdrops

Sprites Pane
Select which of your sprites you want to add code or sound to in this area.

List of Commands
Find the blocks you need by matching the colour to the category name. For example, dark blue blocks will be found in the motion category.

Sprite Library
Choose ready-made sprites for your programs.

Ballerina-c | Ballerina-d | Balloon1-a
Bananas | Baseball | Basketball

Code | Costumes | Sounds

costume3

Paint Editor
This is where you can draw your own sprites or backdrops.

Costume Pane

Drawing Tools

Following Instructions

We'll start off by looking at how a simple robot can be programmed to carry out a series of steps one after another.

This is called a sequential program. In case you don't have a robot handy, we'll be drawing one and creating a maze for it to travel through.

STEP 1 - Remove the cat

duplicate
delete
export

Right-click on the cat and click **delete**.

STEP 2 - Add a sprite

Hover over the **Choose a Sprite** button.

Paint

Click the **Brush** icon.

For help go to: www.maxw.com

STEP 3 - Start drawing

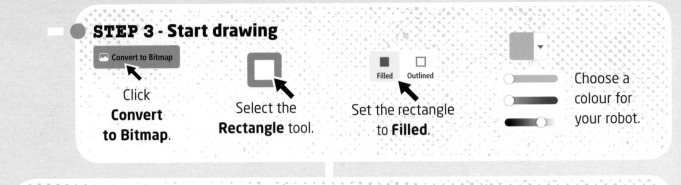

Convert to Bitmap

Click **Convert to Bitmap**.

Select the **Rectangle** tool.

Filled   Outlined

Set the rectangle to **Filled**.

Choose a colour for your robot.

STEP 4 - Draw the robot

Start by dragging out a rectangle in the centre of the drawing area. Make it about one quarter of the width of the drawing area. (We'll draw it quite large so we can add detail, then shrink it in step 8.)

Select a darker colour.

Create two more rectangles to be the robot's arms.

STEP 5 - Eyes and details

Choose white, then draw two white rectangles to start creating the eyes.

Select black, then add pupils to the eyes.

Add any other details you want to your robot.

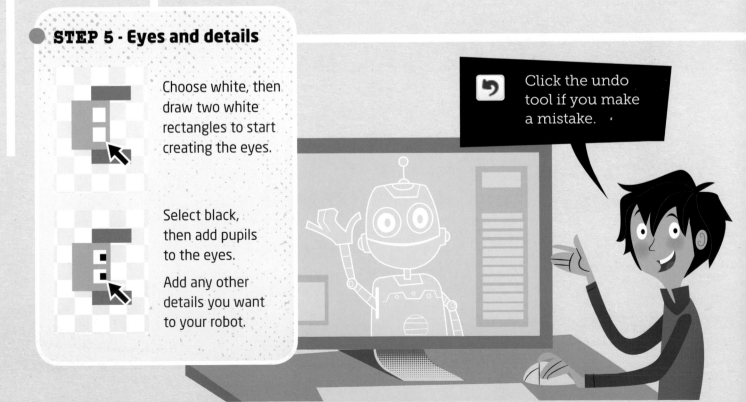

Click the undo tool if you make a mistake.

7

STEP 6 - The maze

Click on the **Stage** icon next to the sprites pane.

Stage

Backdrops

✏ Backdrops

Click the **Backdrops** tab.

🖼 Convert to Bitmap

Click **Convert to Bitmap**.

STEP 7 - Draw some walls

Click the **Line** tool.

25

Make the line thicker.

Choose dark green.

Use the mouse to draw four walls to contain the maze.

Now add a couple of internal walls to make a very simple maze.

Don't worry if the robot looks too big for the maze - your code will make it shrink to fit.

STEP 8 - Add a target

Click the **Choose a Sprite** button.

Laptop

Scroll through to find the **Laptop** sprite and click on it.

STEP 9 - In position

Drag the laptop to the top right corner of the maze.

This will make sure that you are assigning code to control the robot.

STEP 10 - Select the robot

Sprite 1   Laptop

Click on the robot to select it.

If the robot is too big, try changing the code to set its size to 30 or 40 per cent.

STEP 11 - Code it

Code

Click the **Code** tab, then add this code to make the robot reach the laptop.

Code block	Explanation
when 🏳 clicked	Run this code when the green flag is clicked:
set size to **50** %	Shrink the robot down to half its size.
go to x: **-190** y: **-135**	Start at the bottom left of the screen.
point in direction **0▾**	Point upwards.
repeat **240**	Repeat the following code 240 times:
move **1** steps	Move one step forward.
point in direction **90▾**	Point to the right.
repeat **320**	Repeat the following code 320 times:
move **1** steps	Move one step forward.

🏳 **Click the flag to test your code.**
Your robot should slowly move up, then to the right until it reaches the laptop.

Move the laptop sprite to a different part of the maze.

Now move it a little further.

Now click on the robot, and change the code to make it reach the laptop in its new position.

Change the code again to make the robot reach the laptop.

Keep moving the laptop to a new place, then change the code to make the robot find its target.

How it works – moving and turning

Some robots have legs, but most have wheels. Some have caterpillar tracks over their wheels to be able to drive on rough terrain. Wheeled robots usually have two motors, one to drive the wheels onthe left and one to drive the wheels on the right.

To make the robot move forward, both sets of motors need to turn clockwise. To make it reverse, both motors turn anti-clockwise.

To turn left or right, the motors need to turn in opposite directions. To turn left the left-hand side motor turns clockwise, and the right-hand side turns anti-clockwise. To turn right they do the opposite.

Change your maze by adding more walls. Modify your code so the robot still reaches its target - the laptop.

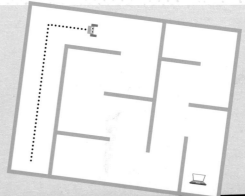

Download more maze backgrounds at www.maxw.com

Sensors

So far our robot has not shown much intelligence. It only found its way through the maze because a prewritten program told it which way to turn and how far to go.

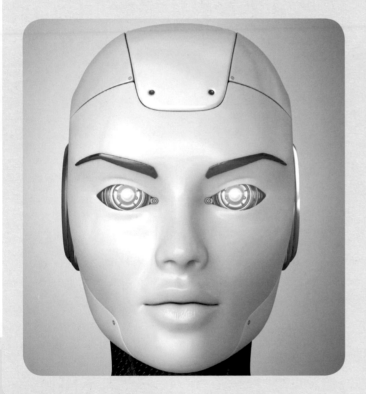

There are many ways to make a robot more useful. One important method is to make the robot more aware of its surroundings. We, as human beings, do this through our five senses. Robots use special components called 'sensors' to try to detect what is near them.

We can change the code in our maze program to make the robot find its own way. By adding code to make it 'sense' where the walls are, it will be able to make choices about when to change direction.

The robot will also need some rules to help it get through the maze. A method called the 'left-hand rule' instructs the robot to try to 'touch' the left-hand side of the maze as it moves. A rule in a program such as this one is called an algorithm.

Sensing the Way

We are going to make a program that can guide a robot through a maze.

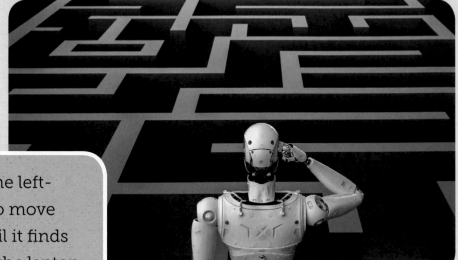

It will use the left-hand rule to move around until it finds its target — the laptop.

STEP 1 - A robot

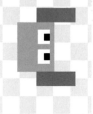

We need a robot. Use the previous program or follow the instructions on pages 6-7 to draw a new one.

STEP 2 - Add a sensor

The robot will need to check if its left arm is touching the wall. Let's make its left arm act like a sensor.

Click the **Costumes** tab.

Select the **Fill** tool.

Choose orange.

Colour the robot's left arm orange.

STEP 3 - Add a target

Click the **Choose a Sprite** button.

Laptop

Scroll through to find the **Laptop** sprite and click on it.

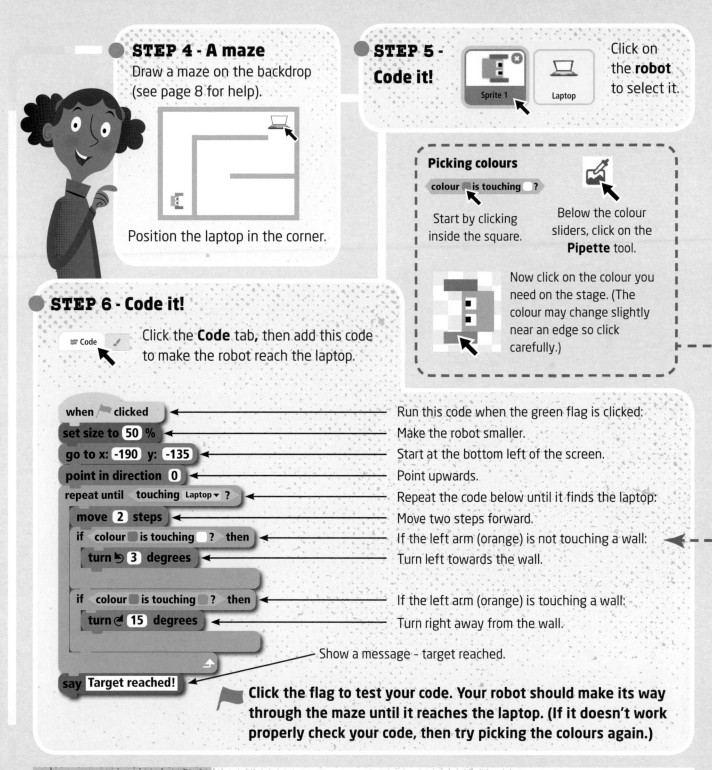

STEP 4 - A maze

Draw a maze on the backdrop (see page 8 for help).

Position the laptop in the corner.

STEP 5 - Code it!

Sprite 1   Laptop

Click on the **robot** to select it.

Picking colours

colour ⬜ is touching ⬜ ?

Start by clicking inside the square.

Below the colour sliders, click on the **Pipette** tool.

Now click on the colour you need on the stage. (The colour may change slightly near an edge so click carefully.)

STEP 6 - Code it!

🖊 Code

Click the **Code** tab, then add this code to make the robot reach the laptop.

```
when 🏴 clicked
set size to 50 %
go to x: -190 y: -135
point in direction 0
repeat until    touching Laptop ▾ ?
    move 2 steps
    if  colour ⬜ is touching ⬜ ?   then
        turn ↰ 3 degrees

    if  colour ⬜ is touching ⬜ ?   then
        turn ↱ 15 degrees

say Target reached!
```

Run this code when the green flag is clicked:
Make the robot smaller.
Start at the bottom left of the screen.
Point upwards.
Repeat the code below until it finds the laptop:
Move two steps forward.
If the left arm (orange) is not touching a wall:
Turn left towards the wall.

If the left arm (orange) is touching a wall:
Turn right away from the wall.

Show a message - target reached.

Click the flag to test your code. Your robot should make its way through the maze until it reaches the laptop. (If it doesn't work properly check your code, then try picking the colours again.)

Investigate

Move the laptop around in the maze. Can the robot still find it?

Try drawing a different shaped maze - how does the robot manage?

What happens if you change the amount the robot turns when it finds a wall or some space?

Can you make the robot move faster? Does it still find its target?

Taking Orders

Robots can be programed to do lots of different tasks.

In this activity we will draw a robot and program it to do a number of different tasks including shaking its head, waving and speaking.

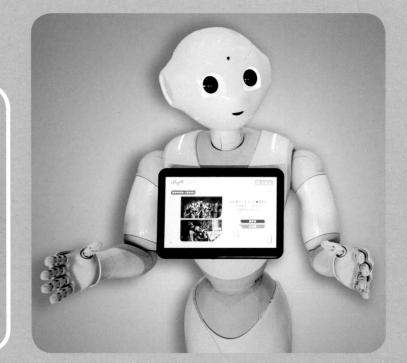

STEP 1 - Remove the cat

duplicate
delete
export

Spri

Right-click on the cat and click **delete**.

STEP 2 - Add a sprite

Paint

Hover over the **Choose a Sprite** button.

Click the **Brush** icon.

For help go to:
www.**maxw**.com

STEP 3 - Start drawing

🖼 Convert to Bitmap

Click **Convert to Bitmap**.

Select the **Rectangle** tool.

■ Filled   ☐ Outlined

Set the rectangle to **Filled**.

Choose a colour for your robot.

STEP 4 - Draw the head

Start by dragging out a rectangle about one quarter of the width of the drawing area in the centre.

Choose orange.

Create a rectangle to be the mouth.

Select the **Ellipse** tool.

Hold down the shift key while you draw to make perfect circles.

Drag out two yellow circles for eyes.

Add pupils to the eyes.

Finally, add any finishing touches to the robot's head.

STEP 5 - Draw the body

Paint

Make another sprite (see step 2).

Convert to Bitmap

Click **Convert to Bitmap**.

Select the **Rectangle** tool.

Choose a colour for the robot's body.

Draw the main part of the body so it takes up about one third of the height of the drawing area.

Then draw the legs.

Add any extra details.

Once you have completed the body and legs, click on the head and drag it onto the body so they line up.

STEP 6 - Draw the right arm

Paint — Make another sprite.

Convert to Bitmap — Click **Convert to Bitmap**.

Select the **Rectangle** tool.

Starting in the centre of the drawing area, drag out a simple rectangle for the arm.

The arm needs to pivot here. We need to make sure we start drawing the arm in the centre of the drawing area.

STEP 7 - Draw the left arm

Repeat the first part of step 6 to make another arm sprite.

This time start in the centre, but drag towards the left to draw the arm.

You should have four sprites now, like this:

Sprite1 Sprite2 Sprite3 Sprite4

Drag the sprites around so they line up properly and your robot looks like this.

STEP 8 - Code it!

Click **Sprite1** to select the head sprite.

Code — Click the **Code** tab then add this code:

when 🏴 clicked	Run this code when the green flag is clicked:
forever	Keep repeating the following code forever:
ask Give me an instruction and wait	Ask the program user to type in an instruction.
if answer = shake then	If the user types in 'shake,' then run this code:
point in direction 95	Tilt the head slightly to the right.
repeat 5	Repeat the following code 5 times:
turn ↺ 10 degrees	Rotate to the left 10 degrees.
wait 0.1 secs	Wait for a moment (1/10 of a second).
turn ↻ 10 degrees	Rotate to the right 10 degrees.
wait 0.1 secs	Wait for a moment (1/10 of a second).
point in direction 90	Straighten the head.
	Keep on looping.

Click the green flag to run your code. Try typing in 'shake' then press the Enter key on the keyboard.

The robot should shake his head!

STEP 9 - Add a sound

🔊 Sounds

Click the **Sounds** tab.

Click **Choose a sound**.

Computer ...

Click **Computer Beep**.

STEP 10 - Change your code

Code

Click the **Code** tab, then add this code at the bottom, just before the end of the 'forever' loop block.

if answer = beep then

start sound Computer Beep ▼

If the user types in 'beep' then run this code:

Play the Computer Beep sound effect.

Click the green flag to test your code. Try typing in 'beep', press Enter and see what happens.

Now let's give the robot a voice by recording some sound. You'll need a microphone to be able to do this. There may already be one built into your computer.

To let Scratch use your microphone you need to click the 'Allow' button when you start recording.

✅ **Allow**

Beware of other websites asking to use your microphone – check with an adult first.

STEP 11 - Robot speech

(•)) Sounds

Click the
Sounds tab.

Hover over the
Choose a Sound
button.

Record

Click
Record.

Record Sound

Record

Click the **Record
button** then say **'Hello'**.

Stop

Save

Press **Stop** and
then **Save**.

Your voice will be shown as a sound
wave like this. Let's add a special
effect – the robot one is great!

If no sound wave appears and you can't
hear anything, make sure the microphone
is selected and turned up by checking the
settings program on your computer.

Robot

STEP 12 - Update your code

Code

As with step 10, we need to insert some code to instruct the robot to make a sound.
Click the **Code** tab. Add this code at the bottom, just before the end of the 'forever'
loop block:

if   answer = hello   then   ◄————————————   If the user types in 'hello' then run this code:

start sound recording1▼   ◄————————————   Play the sound recording.

**Click the green flag to test your code. Try typing in
hello, press Enter and see what happens.**

Investigate

What happens if you
change the number of
degrees turned from
10 to 20 in step 8?

Alter the amount of time in
the 'wait' command block
from 0.1 to 0.01. How does
this change things?

Try changing the number
of times the code repeats
from 5 to 10 in step 8.
What happens?

STEP 13 - Ask the robot to wave

To make the robot wave we need to get the head sprite to send a message to one arm sprite.

broadcast message1 ▼

Find the
broadcast block.

broadcast message1 ▼

Click **New
message**.

New message

✓ message1

New Message

New message name:

wave

Cancel   OK

Type in **wave,** then click **OK**.

Now we need to insert some code to instruct the robot to send the wave message.
Add this code at the bottom, just before the end of the 'forever' loop block:

if   answer = wave ** then** ◄———— If the user types in 'wave', then run this code:

broadcast wave ▼ ◄———— Send the wave message.

STEP 14 - Teach it to wave

Sprite1   Sprite2   Sprite3   Sprite4

In the **Sprites Pane**, click
Sprite3 (the right arm) to
select it. Drag in this code:

when I receive wave ▼ ◄———— When the wave message is received run this code:

repeat 5 ◄———— Repeating the following code 5 times:

turn ↺ 15 **degrees** ◄———— Rotate the arm 15 degrees anti-clockwise.

wait 0.1 **secs** ◄———— Wait for a tenth of a second.

turn ↻ 15 **degrees** ◄———— Rotate the arm 15 degrees clockwise.

wait 0.1 **secs** ◄———— Wait for a tenth of a second.

🚩 **Test your code!**

Code Challenge

Make the robot play other sounds such as new recorded
sounds when you type different commands.
Don't forget to change the code after adding
new sounds to your project.

Can you teach it to wave both arms?
You will need to send a new message to both arms.

Teach the robot to wink. Add a second costume
to the robot's head and change one of the eyes.
What else can you make the robot do?

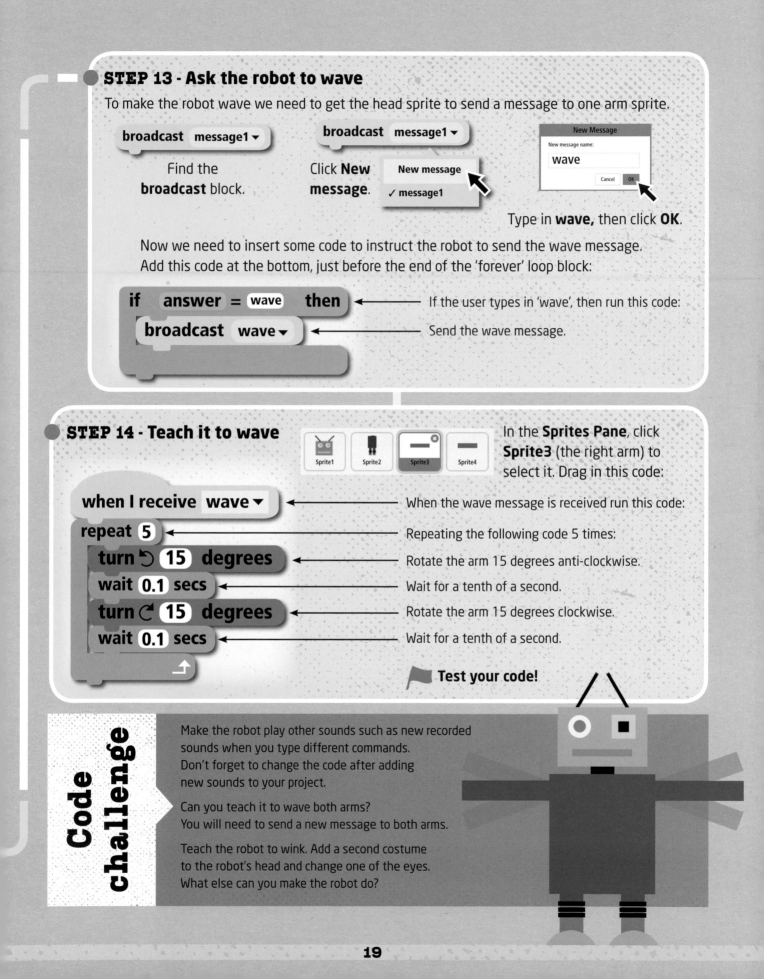

19

The Robot Arm

There are lots of things that a robot can do – even if it only has one arm. Robot arms are used in manufacturing, helping to make all sorts of things from cars to tiny electrical components.

Robot arms can be used to do things that might be dangerous, such as handling hot or dangerous chemicals. They are even used by doctors in operations. Let's find out more by creating our own robot arm with code.

STEP 1 - A robot

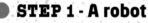

Right-click on the cat and click **delete**.

STEP 2 - Add a sprite

Hover over the **Choose a Sprite** button.

Click the **Brush** icon.

Click **Convert to Bitmap**.

STEP 3 - Zoom in!

To make it easier to draw the robotic hand, click the **Zoom In** button 5 or 6 times to get a closer view.

The drawing area should now look like this. The cross shows the exact centre of the sprite.

STEP 4 - Draw the hand

Choose the **Rectangle** tool.

Filled   Outlined

Set it to **Filled**.

Choose a colour for the wrist.

Drag out a rectangle, which will act as the wrist for the hand.

Click the **Zoom Out** button twice so you have room to draw the fingers.

Click the **Line** tool.

Choose a colour for the fingers.

15

Make the line a little thicker.

Draw four lines to make the two fingers.

So far in this book we have drawn sprites with the mouse, then moved them around with code. As the robot arm has two joints that rotate, it will be hard to keep them both lined up if we use sprites. We will therefore draw the robot arm with code.

STEP 5 - Arm angle

To make the arm move, we need the code to draw it pointing in different directions. The direction it points in will be stored in a variable.

Code

Click the **Code** tab.

Operators

Variables

Click the **Variables** category.

Make a Variable

Click **Make a Variable.**

New variable

New variable name:

arm

● For all sprites   ○ For this sprite only

More Options ▾

Cancel   OK

Type **arm**.

Click **OK**.

For help go to:
www.maxw.com

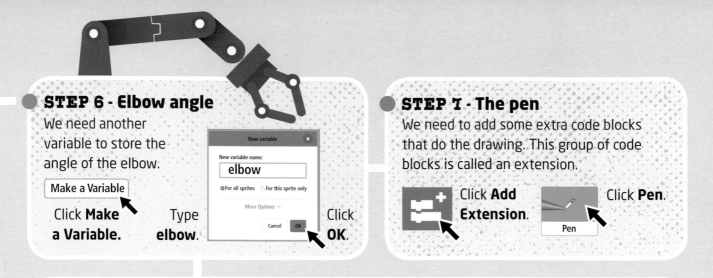

STEP 6 - Elbow angle

We need another variable to store the angle of the elbow.

[Make a Variable]

Click **Make a Variable.**   Type **elbow**.

New variable

New variable name:

elbow

◉ For all sprites   ○ For this sprite only

More Options ▾

Cancel   OK

Click **OK**.

STEP 7 - The pen

We need to add some extra code blocks that do the drawing. This group of code blocks is called an extension.

Click **Add Extension**.   Click **Pen**.

Pen

STEP 8 - Code it!

Drag in this code to draw the robot arm.

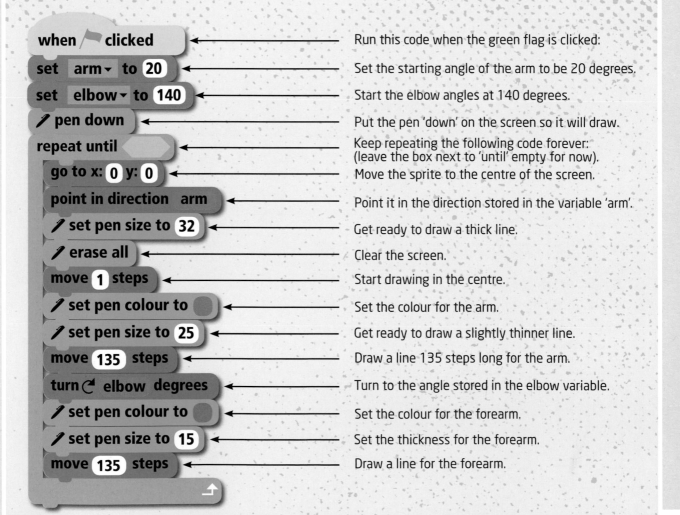

when ⚑ clicked	Run this code when the green flag is clicked:
set arm ▾ to 20	Set the starting angle of the arm to be 20 degrees.
set elbow ▾ to 140	Start the elbow angles at 140 degrees.
✎ pen down	Put the pen 'down' on the screen so it will draw.
repeat until	Keep repeating the following code forever: (leave the box next to 'until' empty for now).
go to x: 0 y: 0	Move the sprite to the centre of the screen.
point in direction arm	Point it in the direction stored in the variable 'arm'.
✎ set pen size to 32	Get ready to draw a thick line.
✎ erase all	Clear the screen.
move 1 steps	Start drawing in the centre.
✎ set pen colour to	Set the colour for the arm.
✎ set pen size to 25	Get ready to draw a slightly thinner line.
move 135 steps	Draw a line 135 steps long for the arm.
turn ↻ elbow degrees	Turn to the angle stored in the elbow variable.
✎ set pen colour to	Set the colour for the forearm.
✎ set pen size to 15	Set the thickness for the forearm.
move 135 steps	Draw a line for the forearm.

⚑ **Click the flag to test your code. It should draw the robot arm with the hand at the end.**

STEP 9 - The code

Let's add code to make the arm move.
Pressing different keys will make the arm or the elbow rotate.

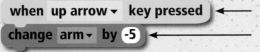

when up arrow ▾ **key pressed** ◄— When the up arrow key is pressed, run this code:

change arm ▾ **by** -5 ◄— Subtract 5 from the value of the 'arm' variable.

when down arrow ▾ **key pressed** ◄— When the down arrow key is pressed, run this code:

change arm ▾ **by** 5 ◄— Add 5 to the value of the 'arm' variable.

when left arrow ▾ **key pressed** ◄— When the left arrow key is pressed, run this code:

change elbow ▾ **by** -5 ◄— Subtract 5 from the value of the 'elbow' variable.

when right arrow ▾ **key pressed** ◄— When the right arrow key is pressed, run this code:

change elbow ▾ **by** 5 ◄— Increase the value of the 'elbow' variable by 5.

🚩 **Click the flag to test your code. Pressing the arrow keys will rotate the arm and the elbow joint, moving the robot arm around. Take some time to get used to how the keys work.**

How it works — the robot arm

Robot arms are made of separate sections, rather like the bones in our body. Instead of using muscles to move, robot arms have special motors called servos that rotate each section. Our robot arm only has two sections, but real robot arms may have six or seven.

A robot arm's fingers or hands often have sensors that can tell when it is gripping something.

Our robot arm is controlled by pressing different keys. Real robot arms are connected to computers that switch the servos on and off to move them. Most have dedicated programs that store when to activate each servo to carry out particular jobs.

Robot Arm Game

We will now add some code to the robot arm to turn it into a game. Apples will appear in random positions. See how many you can grab in one minute!

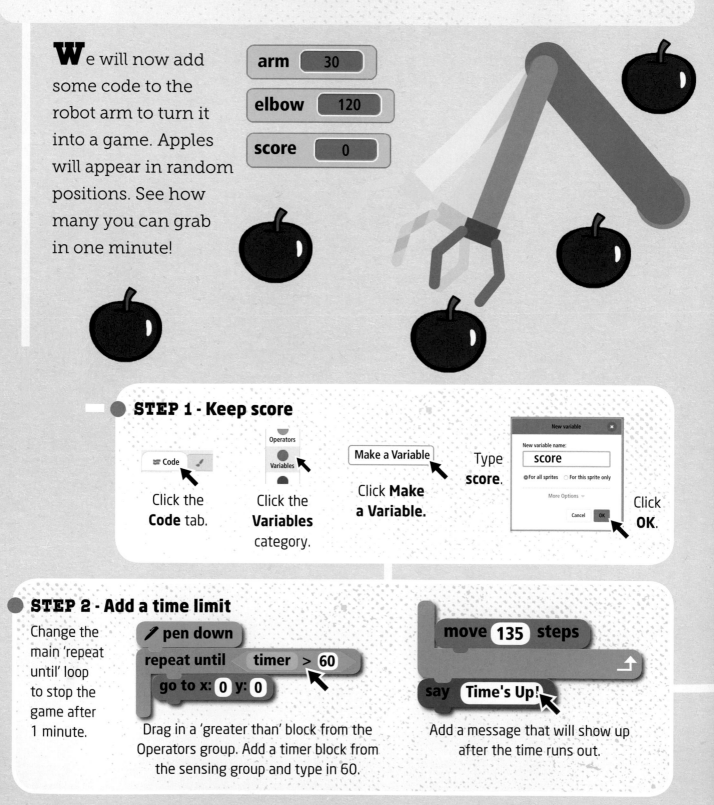

arm	30
elbow	120
score	0

STEP 1 - Keep score

Operators

Code

Variables

Make a Variable

Type **score**.

New variable

New variable name:

score

○ For all sprites   ○ For this sprite only

More Options

Cancel   OK

Click the **Code** tab.

Click the **Variables** category.

Click **Make a Variable.**

Click **OK**.

STEP 2 - Add a time limit

Change the main 'repeat until' loop to stop the game after 1 minute.

    pen down

repeat until   timer > 60

    go to x: 0 y: 0

Drag in a 'greater than' block from the Operators group. Add a timer block from the sensing group and type in 60.

move 135 steps

say   Time's Up!

Add a message that will show up after the time runs out.

24

STEP 3 - Add an apple

Click the **Choose a Sprite** button.

Scroll through to find the **Apple** sprite and click on it.

STEP 4 - Draw the ground

Code

Click on the **Code** tab, then drag in this code to control the apple.

when 🚩 clicked ◄————————— Run this code when the green flag is clicked:

set score ▾ to 0 ◄————————— Reset the score variable to zero.

set size to 50 % ◄————————— Shrink the apple to half its normal size.

forever ◄————————— Repeat the following code forever:

  go to random position ▾ ◄————————— Move the apple to a random place.

  wait until touching Sprite1 ▾ ? ◄————————— Wait until the robot hand grabs the apple.

  change score ▾ by 1 ◄————————— Increase the score by one.

  start sound pop ▾ ◄————————— Play a sound effect.

🚩 **Click the flag to test your game. Use the arrow keys to move the hand around and grab the apples.**

Investigate

Vary the value by which the arm and elbow variables are changed when keys are pressed on page 23, step 9. How does this affect the way the hand moves?

In the main code (page 22, step 8) change 135 to another number. What does this do to the robot arm?

Code challenge

Change the apple to a different object.

Add a variable called 'wrist' that controls the angle of the hand. Update the command keys and main code so the hand can be controlled by other keys.

Adapt the code so the apple is picked up by the hand and moves with it. You could make another variable called 'picked up'. Set it to 'no' at the start. When the hand touches the apple, change this variable to 'yes'. Add a new loop that checks to see if the value of 'picked up' is 'yes'. If it is, then use a code block to move the apple with the hand.

The last challenge is quite tricky! You need to be experienced at using Scratch and variables to succeed!

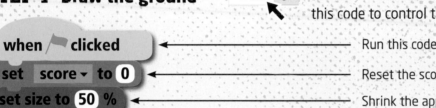

25

Walking and Talking

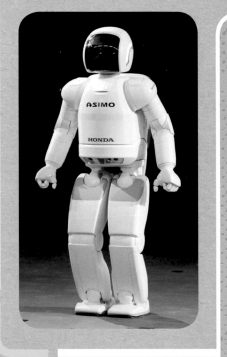

Robots are growing increasingly similar to humans. One of the most advanced robots was developed by Honda, and is known as Asimo.

It is 1.3 m tall and has cameras instead of eyes. Asimo is able to walk and understand simple voice commands. It is even capable of climbing stairs, dancing, opening bottles and playing football!

Asimo has a complex set of motorised servos, mechanical parts, electronics and code. It has gyroscopes and sensors to help it balance and interact with the world.

Let's create a very simple walking robot using animation and some basic voice control.

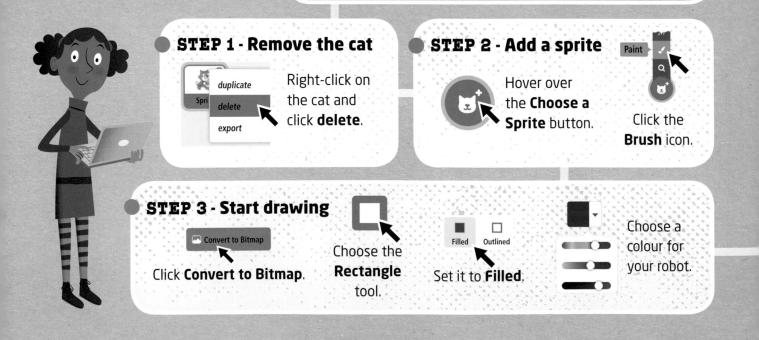

STEP 1 - Remove the cat
Right-click on the cat and click **delete**.

duplicate
delete
export

STEP 2 - Add a sprite
Hover over the **Choose a Sprite** button.

Paint

Click the **Brush** icon.

STEP 3 - Start drawing
Click **Convert to Bitmap**.

Convert to Bitmap

Choose the **Rectangle** tool.

Filled   Outlined

Set it to **Filled**.

Choose a colour for your robot.

STEP 4 - Head and body

Drag out a small rectangle to be the body. Start it in the middle of the drawing area, going up.

Add a head.

And a neck.

Because we are drawing it side-on we will only see one eye.

Click the undo tool if you make a mistake.

Make sure your robot is about 1/3 of the height of the drawing area.

Your robot needs to be in the centre of the drawing area, going up. If you need to move it, use the select tool to draw round it. Now click on the robot and drag it into position.

STEP 5 - How fast?

We now need a speed variable to store how fast the robot is moving. (If it is standing still its speed will be zero.)

Operators

Variables

Click the **Code** tab.

Click the **Variables** category.

Make a Variable

Click **Make a Variable.**

Type **speed**.

New variable

New variable name:

speed

For all sprites   For this sprite only

More Options

Cancel   OK

Click **OK**.

STEP 6 - Stop and go

Drag in this code to make the robot stop or start when the space bar is pressed:

when space ▾ key pressed ← When the space bar is pressed, run this code:

set speed ▾ to 3 - speed ← Set the speed to 3 or 0.

STEP 7 - Main code

Drag in this code to keep the robot moving.

when 🏴 **clicked** ◄————————— When the green flag is clicked run this code:

set rotation style left - right ▾ ◄————————— Set the way the robot looks when it reaches the edge.

set speed ▾ to 0 ◄————————— Start with a speed of zero.

forever ◄————————— Keep repeating this code forever:

move speed steps ◄————————— Move forward if the speed is not zero.

if on edge, bounce ◄————————— If it reaches the edge of the screen, bounce and start moving back the other way.

STEP 8 - Add a leg

Paint Click the **Brush** icon to make a new sprite.

🖼 **Convert to Bitmap** Click **Convert to Bitmap**.

Choose the **Rectangle** tool.

We need to draw the leg in the centre to make sure it pivots correctly.

Draw a small rectangle. Start in the centre of the drawing area, and move down.

Draw a second rectangle at the bottom to create a foot.

STEP 9 - Move the leg

🖌 **Code** Click the **Code** tab. Drag in the following code to get the leg moving back and forth.

when 🏴 **clicked** ◄————————— When the green flag is clicked run this code:

forever ◄————————— Repeat the following code forever:

point in direction 90 ▾ ◄————————— Start with the leg straight.

repeat 10 ▾ ◄————————— Repeat this code 10 times:

go to Sprite1 ▾ ◄————————— Move the leg to Sprite1 (the robot's body).

turn ↺ speed degrees ◄————————— Rotate the leg anti-clockwise. (Using the speed variable means it only turns if the body is moving.)

repeat 10 ▾ ◄————————— Repeat this code 10 times:

go to Sprite1 ▾ ◄————————— Move the leg to Sprite1 (the robot's body).

turn ↻ speed degrees ◄————————— Rotate the leg clockwise. (Using the speed variable means it only turns if the body is moving.)

STEP 10 - Add another leg

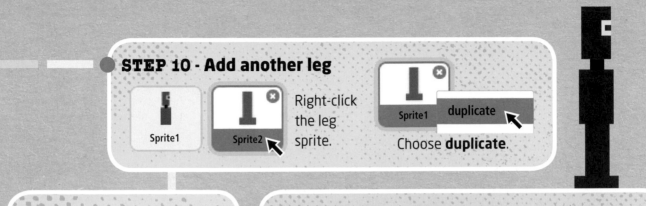

Right-click the leg sprite.

Choose **duplicate**.

STEP 11 - Swap direction

When you duplicate the leg, the code will be duplicated too. But we need this leg to move in the opposite direction to the first leg. To do this, swap around the two 'turn' blocks as shown below:

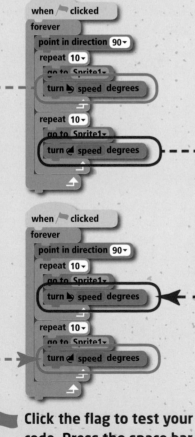

```
when ⚑ clicked
forever
  point in direction 90▾
  repeat 10▾
    go to Sprite1▾
    turn ↻ speed degrees
  repeat 10▾
    go to Sprite1▾
    turn ↺ speed degrees
```

```
when ⚑ clicked
forever
  point in direction 90▾
  repeat 10▾
    go to Sprite1▾
    turn ↻ speed degrees
  repeat 10▾
    go to Sprite1▾
    turn ↺ speed degrees
```

⚑ **Click the flag to test your code. Press the space bar to see your robot walk across the screen!**

STEP 12 - Voice control!

There is a quick way to make the robot move when it hears a sound using a microphone. Add this code, then try clapping your hands to make it move or stop. Try saying 'stop' or 'go' and see what happens!

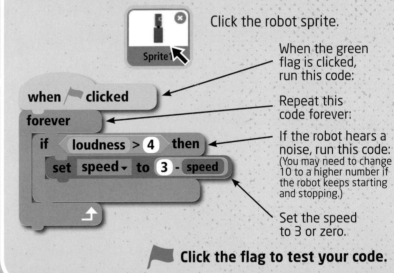

Click the robot sprite.

```
when ⚑ clicked
forever
  if  loudness > 4  then
    set speed▾ to 3 - speed
```

When the green flag is clicked, run this code:

Repeat this code forever:

If the robot hears a noise, run this code:
(You may need to change 10 to a higher number if the robot keeps starting and stopping.)

Set the speed to 3 or zero.

⚑ **Click the flag to test your code.**

Our robot doesn't really understand what you say - it just tests whether there is any sound being made. For it to comprehend different words it would need to analyse the sound in more detail.

See the tips at the bottom of page 17 for help with using the microphone.

Bugs and Debugging

If you find your code isn't working as expected, stop and look through each command you have put in. Think about what you want it to do, and what it is really telling the computer to do. If you are entering one of the programs in this book, check you have not missed a line. Some things to check:

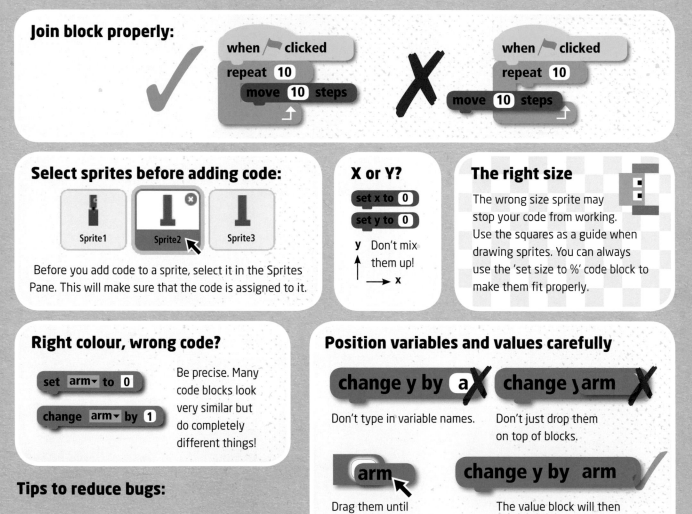

Join block properly:

when ⚑ clicked
repeat 10
move 10 steps ✓

when ⚑ clicked
repeat 10
move 10 steps ✗

Select sprites before adding code:

Sprite1 Sprite2 Sprite3

Before you add code to a sprite, select it in the Sprites Pane. This will make sure that the code is assigned to it.

X or Y?

set x to 0
set y to 0

y Don't mix them up!
→ x

The right size

The wrong size sprite may stop your code from working. Use the squares as a guide when drawing sprites. You can always use the 'set size to %' code block to make them fit properly.

Right colour, wrong code?

set arm to 0
change arm by 1

Be precise. Many code blocks look very similar but do completely different things!

Position variables and values carefully

change y by a ✗   change y arm ✗

Don't type in variable names.   Don't just drop them on top of blocks.

arm   change y by arm ✓

Drag them until a circle appears.   The value block will then snap into place.

Tips to reduce bugs:

• When things are working properly spend time looking through your code so you understand each line.
Experiment and change your code, try out different values.
To be good at debugging you need to understand what each code block does and how your code works.

• Practice debugging! Make a very short program and get a friend to change one block only, while you aren't looking. Can you fix it?

• If you are making your own program, spend time drawing a diagram and planning it before you start. Try changing values if things don't work, and don't be afraid to start again - you will learn from it.

Glossary

AI (artificial intelligence) - software that does more than just follow steps. AI systems respond with apparent intelligence to outside events.

Algorithm - rules or steps followed to make something work or complete a task.

Bug - an error in a program that stops it working properly.

Code block - a draggable instruction icon used in Scratch.

Conditional - a block of code that only runs if something is true.

Debug - removing bugs (or errors) from a program.

Degrees - the units used to measure angles.

Gyroscope - an instrument with a turning wheel, mounted on an axis that can turn in any direction.

Icon - a small clickable image on a computer.

Loop - repeating one or more commands a number of times.

Random - a number that can't be predicted.

Right click - clicking the right mouse button on a sprite or icon.

Sensor - a device that measures something in the real world, such as the temperature, and sends it to a computer as a value.

Sequence - commands that are run one after another in order.

Servo - a special motor in a robot that can turn very accurately.

Software - a computer program containing instructions written in code.

Sprite - an object with a picture on it that moves around the stage.

Stage - the place in Scratch that sprites move around on.

Steps - small movements made by sprites.

System - a combination of software, hardware, sensors and information.

Variable - a value used to store information in a program that can change.

Index

FURTHER INFORMATION

Gifford, Clive. *Get Ahead in Computing* series. Wayland, London, UK: 2017.

Wood, Kevin. *Project Code* series. Franklin Watts, London, UK: 2017

Wainewright, Max. *Generation Code: I'm an Advanced Scratch Coder.* Wayland, London, UK: 2017.